I LIKE IT WHEN . . .

Sept 1998
To MUMPS

Kelsie & Vicki Yohe

First Steck-Vaughn Edition 1992

Copyright © 1990 American Teacher Publications

Published by Steck-Vaughn Company

Library of Congress number: 90-8015

Library of Congress Cataloging in Publication Data.

Auster, Benjamin.
  I like it when... /by Benjamin Auster; illustrated by Marsha Winborn.

  (Ready-set-read)
  Summary: A boy describes the joys and problems involved in doing things with his family.
  [1. Family life—Fiction.] I. Winborn, Marsha, ill. II. Title. III. Series.
PZ27.A924Iaab   1990   [E]—dc20   90-8015

ISBN 0-8172-3578-7   hardcover library binding

ISBN 0-8114-6742-2   softcover binding

  3 4 5 6 7 8 9 0   96 95 94

READY·SET·READ

I Like It When . . .

by Benjamin Auster
illustrated by Marsha Winborn

RSVP
RAINTREE
STECK-VAUGHN
PUBLISHERS
The Steck-Vaughn Company

Austin, Texas

I like it when I shop with my mother,

except when she says, "Try this on!"

I like it when I cook with my father,

except when he says, "Time to clean up!"

12

I like it when I play with my sister,

except when she says, "I win again!"

I like it when I build with my brother,

except when he says, "Wheeeeeee!"

I like it when I paint all by myself,

Sharing the Joy of Reading

Reading a book aloud to your child is just one way you can help your child experience the joy of reading. Now that you and your child have shared **I Like It When . . .,** you can help your child begin to think and react as a reader by encouraging him or her to:

• Retell or reread the story with you, looking and listening for the repetition of specific letters, sounds, words, or phrases.

• Make a picture of a favorite character, event, or key concept from this book.

• Talk about his or her own ideas or feelings about the characters in this book and other things that the characters might do.

Here is an activity that you can do together to help extend your child's appreciation of this book: You and your child can talk about some of the things you like to do together. Pick one thing that you would both like to do. Then do it!